Echoes of Kotdwar
Between Love and Hatred

Arnav Vibhuti

Ukiyoto Publishing

All global publishing rights are held by

Ukiyoto Publishing

Published in 2024

Content Copyright © Arnav Vibhuti

ISBN 9789364941730

All rights reserved.

No part of this publication may be reproduced, transmitted, or stored in a retrieval system, in any form by any means, electronic, mechanical, photocopying, recording or otherwise, without the prior permission of the publisher.

The moral rights of the author have been asserted.

This is a work of fiction. Names, characters, businesses, places, events, locales, and incidents are either the products of the author's imagination or used in a fictitious manner. Any resemblance to actual persons, living or dead, or actual events is purely coincidental.

This book is sold subject to the condition that it shall not by way of trade or otherwise, be lent, resold, hired out or otherwise circulated, without the publisher's prior consent, in any form of binding or cover other than that in which it is published.

www.ukiyoto.com

To the Kotdwar Railway Station, the beautiful mother nature sorrounding it and the lovable people of the city.

Acknowledgement

This book stands as a heartfelt homage to Kotdwar, the city that has been my guiding star, my inspiration, and my refuge. Kotdwar has not only nurtured me but has become a fundamental part of my being, imparting deep lessons through its diverse experiences, both joyous and challenging.

Each poem in this collection was crafted amidst the clamor of railway stations or during the rhythmic sway of train journeys. These fleeting moments offered the perfect setting for my thoughts to flow, infusing each verse with the essence of movement and transition.

Writing this book has been a long-held dream, a manifestation of my deep love for storytelling and my profound empathy for human emotions. Through these poems, I have strived to capture the subtleties of life as I see them, hoping to touch the hearts of those who read them.

Most importantly, I extend my heartfelt thanks to Kotdwar, whose streets resonate with whispers of inspiration and whose spirit infuses every word in this book. I hope these poems carry a piece of my soul back to the city that has given me so much.

Thank you.
Arnav Vibhuti

CONTENTS

Prologue	1
Chapter - 1	1
Chapter - 2	9
Chapter - 3	13
Chapter – 4	20
Chapter – 5	23
Chapter – 6	27
Chapter – 7	33
Chapter – 8	36
Chapter – 9	40
An Ode To Kotdwar	47
About the Author	48

Prologue

"Echoes of Kotdwar" is an introspective poetry collection exploring the author's tumultuous relationship with Shirin, framed against the city of Kotdwar. The narrative begins with a serendipitous encounter with Shirin, united by their mutual love for literature and an intense emotional bond. This initial friendship evolves into a profound connection, where the author values Shirin's companionship and intellectual exchange. However, complications emerge when the author inadvertently steps into a complex emotional landscape, given Shirin's romantic involvement with Navin. Despite their shared joy, the author's desire for deeper significance creates tension, unaware of Shirin's deep feelings for Navin.

The turning point occurs when Shirin confesses her lasting love for Navin, leaving the author heartbroken and disillusioned. Struggling with self-doubt and diminished self-worth, the author seeks refuge in literature, finding solace and clarity through writing as he embarks on a journey of introspection and healing.

As time passes, Shirin returns, seeking comfort after her breakup with Navin. Though the author offers support and attempts to alleviate her pain, unresolved feelings and lingering jealousy strain their renewed relationship, leading to misunderstandings and further emotional conflict.

Ultimately, the author's journey leads him to self-discovery and growth. Moving to a new environment and embracing solitude, he finds peace and renewal in nature. Despite Shirin's return rekindling old wounds, the author learns to value his independence and self-worth. "Echoes of Kotdwar" captures this emotional voyage, highlighting the city's symbolic role in his path to self-acceptance and fulfillment. The collection stands as a tribute to resilience, self-discovery, and the profound impact of finding solace in unexpected places.

Chapter - 1

I

In the shadows of my turbulent days,
I wrestle with love's thorny maze,
Bound in a relationship's cruel embrace,
Seeking solace in a kinder place.

Through the ether of virtual screens,
Fate guides me to where light convenes,
An online class, unexpected find,
Where Shirin appears, gentle and kind.

In the midst of lectures, my eyes stray,
Captivated by her peaceful display,
Silent smiles and tranquil grace,
Offering me a serene embrace.

Dreams bloom quietly, courage wanes,
Yet my heart yearns, to break free of chains,
To befriend her, to share the unspoken,
In the silence where hope has awoken.

Each glance steals a moment's delight,
A flicker of warmth in the cold of night,
She, an oasis in my stormy sea,
A beacon of calm where my soul longs to be.

In the quiet spaces between our gaze,
A connection blooms, defying the haze,
Of past wounds and fearful doubts,
Love's tender whisper quietly shouts.

Our story unfolds in tender hues,
Of courage found in unlikely views,
In a classroom meant for learning's call,
Two souls find peace amidst it all.

II

In Shirin's verses, emotions bloom like flowers,
Each line a tale of life's deepest hours.
A soul immersed in literature's embrace,
Finding solace in sadness, strength in grace.

Her words, a mirror to the heart's gentle tides,
Reflecting nature's beauty, where love abides.
Intrigued, I seek the essence of her lore,
To understand what shaped her to the core.

Through poetry's lens, her spirit shines bright,
A journey woven with wisdom and light.
In the realm of her life, secrets unfurl,
Revealing the tapestry of this beautiful soul

III

Through the quiet corridors of youth,
Where solitude reigned supreme,
Shirin, a soul of depth and dreams,
With books as her only gleam.

Introvert and tender-hearted,
She found solace in written lore,
Her world of words a sanctuary,
Where her spirit could soar.

No friends to share her days with,
She walked a path alone,
Silent echoes and whispered pages,
Her companions, her own.

Yet in the depths of her longing,
A desire flickered bright,
To bridge the gap of isolation,
To bask in friendship's light.

Then came the day when bonds formed,
Friendships sweetly bloomed,
A circle small, but precious,
Where her heart felt unencumbered, resumed.

But storms can brew in calmest seas,
And strife can tear apart,
One friend's clash, a rift unasked,
Shattered the fragile heart.

Alone again in crowded rooms,
Betrayed by friends once near,
Shirin found solace not in voices,
But in words that held her dear.

Words became her refuge,
Her verses painted pain and grace,
From her pen flowed healing waters,
Kindness her guiding embrace.

Through literature's gentle touch,
She found her voice anew,
Inspiring others to embrace empathy,
In words both old and new.

For in the silence of her journey,
She discovered strength refined,
Shirin, the poet, weaving tales of hope,
For hearts both gentle and kind.

IV

In Shirin's tale of trials deep,
I felt her pain, her sorrows steep.
Through solitude and strife's cruel art,
She found within, a gentle heart.

Her journey shaped by lonely hours,
Yet wisdom bloomed from thorny flowers.
She emerged, a soul refined and true,
Guiding others with grace imbued.

In her presence, a beacon bright,
A guiding star in darkest night.
No less than supernatural, her glow,
Enlightening paths we yearn to know.

In her shadow, I found solace rare,
Her wisdom a balm, beyond compare.
Shirin, a spirit soaring high,
A beautiful person, beneath the sky.

V

In the bond of books and tales we shared,
Shirin and I, hearts open and bared.
Through pages turned and stories told,
Dark pasts softened, futures bold.

Literature, our compass, emotions untold,
Guiding us through humanity's gold.
Across divides of religion and creed,
A friendship blossomed, a rare seed.

Different paths, yet souls aligned,
In discussions deep, our thoughts entwined.
Her free spirit welcomed mine to roam,
In the sanctuary of her heart's home.

In her eyes, I found a mirror clear,
Reflecting hopes, dispelling fear.
A friendship pure, across the miles,
United by stories, laughter, and smiles.

VI

Suddenly in the twilight's hush, a promise left behind,
Shirin's vow echoed, yet she vanished, unkind.
Days slipped into silence, weeks wore thin,
No trace of her presence, no whisper within.

Sadness gripped my heart, apprehension grew,
Did I err, or fail her? The reasons I drew,
Imagined scenarios, a mind in unrest,
Searching through shadows, longing, distressed.

A tumultuous time, fresh wounds from a past,
Traumatic partings lingered, shadows cast.
Loneliness engulfed, amidst confusion's reign,
Shirin, my beacon, lost in the pain.

Tears welled, questions haunted my weary mind,
What wrongs did I commit, fate so unkind?
Yet, amidst despair, a flicker of hope held fast,
Guiding me through the storm, a resilience amassed.

In the quietude of solitude, I found strength anew,
A journey through darkness, searching for you.
For in the echoes of our bond, affection's enduring art,
I wait for your return, Shirin, my missing part.

Chapter - 2

I

In the quiet of a moonlit night, Shirin returned,
After few months' absence, her disappearance burned.
"I was busy with household chores," she sighed,
Ramzan's festival keeping her occupied.

Her words, like arrows, pierced my heart,
For weeks without her felt like we drifted apart.
"I had no time," she said with a fleeting frown,
To think of our talks, to hear me out.

Inconsiderate, I felt, like a forgotten song,
Unnoticed, unimportant, where did I belong?
A year later she would speak of Navin, her joyful confide,
Sharing festive joys with him by her side.

A dagger to my soul, a bittersweet token,
Realizing I was less than she had once spoken.
To feel significant, yet to be unseen,
Such loneliness in the places where friendship had been.

Now I know the pain of insignificance's sting,
In a heart once held high, where echoes now ring.

II

From the depths of hurt, I found my way,
Shirin's return brightened my day.
She, my guiding star, back in sight,
No longer lost in the shadows of night.

With clarity, I asked for space and grace,
To share in her life, to have my place.
She agreed, with a promise in her eyes,
Dreams of togetherness began to rise.

Prepared to cherish, to hold her near,
Inspirations and joys, no room for fear.
For in her presence, I found my truth,
Emotions and freedom, in our youth.

So we walk this path, hearts aligned,
A future envisioned, forever entwined.

III

In the dance of days, Shirin and I found more time,
Conversations blossomed beyond emotions climb.
Hobbies, interests, daily tales unfurled,
Binding us closer in life's vibrant swirl.

She, a collector of moments, capturing all,
Places, foods cherished in memory's thrall.
Closer I felt, yearning for her regard,
Unseen wounds when attention seemed marred.

Silent desires to know her deeper still,
Yet courage faltered, fears to fulfill.
Occasional irritations, mysteries unsolved,
Complications brewed, stress unresolved.

In tangled emotions, where paths divide,
Longing for clarity, hearts open wide.
Navigating complexities, hopes aflame,
In this delicate dance, seeking friend's name.

IV

In the warmth of shared moments, Shirin spoke,
Of Navin, her love, her heart's bespoke.
A poem she penned, love and togetherness bound,
In his song, her sadness found solace profound.

Army man, once a schoolmate dear,
Their story unfolded, love clear.
Blushing, she recounted their fights,
Who loved more, who revived each other's lights.

Her words, a dagger twisting inside,
She denied, yet love she couldn't hide.
Bathing in tears, her smiles cut deep,
No words to speak, heartbroken, I steep.

Yet in the silence, a strange calm crept in,
No more illusions, where dreams had been.
Realization dawned, painful yet clear,
Her heart belonged to another, my dear.

Acceptance brought peace, a bitter sweet tide,
No more daydreams, where secrets hide.
In the echoes of her laughter, I found release,
A chapter closed, a heartache's gentle peace.

Chapter - 3

I

In the quiet of the exam day's start,
Destiny wove us together, though apart.
Shirin and I, linked by a shared past,
Through courses and lessons that couldn't last.

Anxious and eager to be at my seat,
Hoping to glimpse her, our eyes might meet.
I sought about her online, through public domain,
To learn her path, where she might remain.

In the heart's quest, a journey unfolds,
To Kotdwar, where her story holds.
Unknown lands beckon, like Lansdowne's grace,
Serene hills and chilled air embrace.

Train's rhythmic journey, a path to seek,
Through broken roads, fears and mystique.
Arrival in sunlight, nerves held tight,
Her smile, a beacon in love's soft light.

Red suit, blue dupatta in perfect blend,
Matching my T-shirt, as if fate penned.
Nervous silence, our eyes entwine,
Courage found, words in whispers align.

Echoes of Kotdwar

Through Kotdwar's streets, we roam and explore,
Sharing tales and dreams, our hearts adore.
On the platform's edge, moments entwine,
Smiles exchanged, hearts in rhythm divine.

Shirin, so shy, with a smile so bright,
Her laughter filled the day with light.
She seemed quite stern from words we'd shared,
Yet so gentle, soft she appeared.

She brought me a lunch, her joy so sweet,
Her childish goodbye made my day complete.
I watched her fade as my train moved away,
Her smile stayed with me, through out the day.

Departing waves, time's fleeting grace,
Rain blesses the journey, nature's embrace.
Rainbows paint skies, love's colors bloom,
Through train windows, a soul's heirloom.

Homebound trails, where memories ignite,
Her essence lingers, through the night.
In thoughts of her and Kotdwar's embrace,
Bliss erases scars, happiness finds its place.

Once more, joy blooms in heart's delight,
A chapter of friendship, in dreams taking flight.

II

In echoes of whispers, in friendship's glow,
Once dreamed of more, now content to know,
I stood in shadows of what could not be,
Yet found solace in moments, calm and free.

Shirin, a confidant, a guide so dear,
In her words, solace would often appear.
Though not the muse of her heart's delight,
I cherished the bond in the softest light.

Longing drifted, like petals in wind's flight,
Yearning for echoes of emotions bright.
Yet in the quiet of solitude's embrace,
Found peace in memories, a gentle grace.

Through streets I wandered, seeking the past,
Finding beauty in memories that last.
In the tapestry woven, a friend's sweet art,
In the gentle beat of a tranquil heart.

III

In quiet shadows, I dared to pry,
Shirin's life, hidden deep inside.
I sought her story without a sound,
Learning more than her words around.

Silent days passed, my heart concealed,
Knowing more than she revealed.
One evening's truth, in soft moonlight,
Shared my knowing, innocent and right.

But words, once spoken, took their toll,
In her eyes, betrayal took hold,
'A breach of trust, my heart undone',
Her hurtful words, like daggers spun.

I stood bewildered, in the storm's cruel wake,
My innocence lost, my heart did ache,
In the chasm between truth and lie,
Lost friendship's song, a mournful sigh.

I glimpsed her life, unveiled yet bright,
No trespass, just curiosity's flight.
But Shirin, unmoved, her defences tall,
Refused my words, let anger fall.

In digital realms where privacy fades,
Misunderstandings cut like blades.
Yet amidst discord, a truth is sown,
In pixels and bytes, forgiveness is grown.

No fault I claim, just curiosity's quest,
To understand the life she manifests.
But in the circuits cold embrace,
Misunderstandings find no grace.

IV

In the silent hum of ones and zeros, I delved,
Into Shirin's personal life, curiosity compelled.
Yet innocence turned to accusation's sting,
As privacy's breach, to her, I unwittingly bring.

I pleaded, explained, my intentions pure and clear,
To understand, to connect, without a trace of fear.
But her silence grew, a wall of distrust,
Her words unspoken, her heart encased in rust.

Then came the letter, a torrent of pain,
Words laden with hurt, like a relentless rain.
Each line a dagger, each phrase a thorn,
Piercing deep, leaving my soul torn.

"Worst person," she penned, with venomous art,
Accusations unfurled, tearing me apart.
In the echo of her anger, I sought redemption's plea,
But the silence lingered, a chasm between her and me.

In the realm of screens, where emotions abound,
Misunderstandings fester, without a sound.
Yet in her letter's bitterness, a reflection I find,
Of boundaries crossed, and hearts left behind.

V

"Since the day one, I was genuine with you,
Opening my heart despite wounds, so true.
Broken by those who came before,
Yet I trusted you, opened every door.

Address, secrets, fears laid bare,
In your hands, I placed my rarest care.
Believing we were friends, close and tight,
But you shattered trust with cruel insight.

You claimed no one understands your plight,
Yet failed to grasp my soul's gentle light.
Sensitive, you knew, yet made me weep,
Questioning myself in shadows deep.

I thought you compassionate, kind,
An empath, with understanding aligned.
But you proved me wrong in every way,
Choosing betrayal, leading me astray.

Your actions weren't the only choice,

But you preferred to silence my voice.
Now a stranger where a friend once stood,
You triggered pain where healing once could.

I'll learn from this, though hard to bear,
No more trust, no more will I dare.
You are a bitter lesson learned,
In my life's tale, you'll never return.

I hate you for the pain you've sown,
Forcing me to face my tears alone.
Thank you for the harsh words spoken,
For leaving my spirit broken.

Farewell to you, in heart's disdain,
May our paths never cross again."

Chapter – 4

I

In the shadows of whispered doubts, I stand,
Where once warmth dwelled, now icy fingers clasp,
Her words, a tempest, rend my tranquil land,
Accusations hurl, pierce the tenderest grasp.

I gave all I could, from the depths of my soul,
Yet branded the worst, the most hateful by you,
Each deed now a shard, jagged, taking its toll,
In disbelief, I falter, not knowing what to do.

Did my affection not speak in the silence of my acts?
Were my intentions lost in the storm of your pain?
Echoes of your disdain, like relentless impacts,
Leave scars unseen, yet deep, in my heart's domain.

Words unspoken, explanations left unsaid,
Now the chasm widens, a rift in our gaze,
I search her eyes, but find only dread,
As self-doubt shrouds me in a haze.

Where do I stand, in this fractured bond?
Can healing find a way through this shattered trust?
Or must I bear the weight of her judgment's wand,
In solitude's grasp, where dreams turn to dust?

Yet through the ache, a flicker of hope,
That understanding may bridge this great divide,
That love's tender tendrils can help us cope,
And wash away the wounds we can't abide.

For in the deepest ache, there lies a plea,
To reclaim what's lost in the tempest's swell,
To find solace in the truth that sets us free,
And mend the heart's fragile, cherished shell.

II

In shattered pieces, I stand, heart torn,
Care and affection, with love adorned.
Pure intentions met with harsh retort,
Hatred returned my soul distraught.

Surprised by the bitter twist of fate,
Love mirrored back as venomous hate.
Struggling for answers, in the dark I roam,
Trauma's grip, nightmares haunt my home.

Yet I choose to move forward, despite the pain,
Embracing life, though scars remain.
Letting go of anger, forgiving the past,
Accepting the fate that's been cast.

No longer consumed by bitterness' plight,
I release the grudge, surrender the fight.
For in the end, I've found my peace,
With wounds that heal, and heart's release.

Literature embraced me, a comforting embrace,
Poetry and quotes, a refuge, a place,
Where healing began, ink became my voice,
In pages turned, I found my choice.

Writing this book, a journey to mend,
Each word a step, each line a friend,
Through verses and quotes, my soul found release,
In the therapy of words, I found peace.

Chapter – 5

I

After the storm of strife, a long silence ensued,
Shirin, until distant, suddenly returned one day.
Unbelievable, her return, after such deep disdain,
Yet my heart held a soft corner, despite the pain.

She stood before me, wounded and frail,
Her plea for healing, her spirit in travail.
Tears welled in my eyes, seeing her plight,
I embraced her gently, with emotions burning bright.

In her eyes, I saw regret and remorse,
Yet I chose to soothe, not to enforce.
With tender care, I reassured her fears,
Promised to stay, to wipe away her tears.

Together we walked through scars of the past,
Forgiveness bloomed, a bond built to last.
In her healing journey, I began playing my part,
A new chapter unfolded, a mended heart.

II

In the silence of night, Shirin confides in me,
Of loneliness deepened by Navin's departure, so stark.
Her love, her life, soon to be another's embrace,
Leaving her devastated, lost in sorrow's dark.

Sleep eludes her, night after night,
Dark circles under eyes, a testament to her plight.
Thoughts of ending it all, in despair's grip,
Life without Navin, a sinking ship.

Memories haunt her, his absence a void,
She yearns for his touch, now forever denied.
Her heart aches with every breath she takes,
Lost in the past, in love's forsaken wake.

I hold her close, whispering words of hope,
Promising her light beyond this darkened slope.
Together we'll navigate this tempestuous sea,
Till she finds solace again, till she's free.

III

The quiet glow after dinner's embrace,
I crafted words to soften Siri's pain,
A delicate dance in the alien space,
To comfort, to heal, amidst life's strain.

Challenges abound, in forging each line,
Yet excitement surged in this tender task,
Designing dialogues, hoping to refine,
Her spirit weary, yet a soul to unmask.

Emotions entwined, both joy and sorrow,
Navigating her world, a fragile thread,
Through suffocation's shadow, we borrow,
Respect and gratitude, where hearts are led.

Stories woven, shared in twilight's gleam,
A laughter echoed, healing unseen,
In her tough times, a blessing did gleam,
A bond cherished, where hope convenes.

IV

In the stillness of night, she'd wake, trembling with fright,
Nightmares haunting her, in shadows deep and wide.
But I was there, with gentle songs, to soothe her fears away,
My words a beacon of hope, till dawn's first light.

She said my care healed wounds, made her heart anew,
Grateful for my efforts, whispered thanks so true.
In her eyes, a reflection, a ghost from her past,
She saw Navin in me, a love that didn't last.

Emotions stirred, in twilight's soft embrace,
I sang to her, hoping my voice would erase,
The echoes of darkness, that plagued her sleep,
In my songs, she found peace, in dreams so deep.

Chapter – 6

I

In the twilight's gentle glow, Shirin would confide,
Of Navin, her love, and their tender stride.
He sang to her, melodies sweet and true,
Shared special treats, their love anew.

Shy at first, but his touch so bold,
In the narrow streets, their story told.
Whispers of passion, evenings so grand,
Amidst mountains and rivers, hand in hand.

Hashtagged moments, nights they savoured,
Secret getaways, their love flavoured.
In cars, kisses hot as noon,
Nature's embrace, under the moon.

Holiday's passed, tears they'd shed,
As Navin's leave drew to a dread.
Wanted him to quit, leave it all behind,
But duty bound, their hearts entwined.

Together they wept, in love's embrace,
Navigating life, each moment a chase.
For Shirin and Navin, love's sweetest blend,
In memories cherished, forever penned.

II

In their vows, a future promised bright,
Yet life's hand dealt a different plight.
Navin's parents chose a bride with care,
Shirin's heart shattered, in deep despair.

Navin, uneasy with the chosen one,
Accepted her to end what had begun.
Punishing himself, hurting Shirin's core,
They wanted, but the society closed the door.

Marrying out of pity, not love's flame,
As the bride, alone save for her grandma's name.
With heavy hearts, they chose to part,
Shirin sought solace, a fresh new start.

Turning to me for friendship's embrace,
In her eyes, a flicker of hope found place.

III

Unexpectedly, Navin came into my space,
Interrupting moments meant for just us, face to face.
For sympathy, I had no choice but to step aside,
But Feeling insignificant next to his stride.

Learning of his life, their shared romance,
His constant presence, like an unending dance.
Emotions tangled, envy crept in,
Disliking his intrusion, where to begin?

I scrolled through details of his life,
Feeling low, amidst this strife.
As days grew harder, I questioned my role,
In Shirin's world, losing parts of my soul.

Navigating complexities, emotions rough,
Yearning for peace, finding my own rebuff.

IV

Amidst the ebb and flow of my dance with Shirin,
We persevered together, forging ahead boldly.
Shirin, petite and slender, yet filled with grace,
Her hair a soft wave, her neck a fragrant embrace.

Her cheeks tender, lips gentle and kind,
In the nature's laps, emotions intertwined.
Exploring Shirin's sensuality, her physical allure,
Thoughts of Navin intrude, emotions obscure.

Stress mounts, tears blur my sight,
Angst for Navin clouds my light.
Struggling to find peace amid the storm,
Hiding emotions from Shirin, keeping her warm.

Navigating complexities, tides of emotion,
In the dance with Shirin, finding devotion.
Amidst ups and downs, our journey ahead,
In this tangled web where hearts are led.

V

Less mature than Shirin, I stumbled through mistakes,
Unaware of their gravity, each one a lesson to take.
Yet, I owned my faults, never let them repeat,
Open to her guidance, where correction could meet.

But some struggles persisted, like envy's tight hold,
Irritation for Navin, his past untold.
One afternoon, her words cut deep like a knife,
"I don't want you in my life," ending our strife.

Shirin took my uncomfort as doubt,
Questions about Navin made her left out.
Misunderstanding led her to part ways,
Leaving me alone with my words in a daze.

Desperate pleas, attempts to mend,
Her resolve firm, my heart couldn't defend.
Too timid to hold her, to ask her to stay,
Courage eluded, as she slipped away.

VI

In the quiet of dusk, I chose to leave,
Shirin's smile faded, no longer a reprieve.
More storms than sun, our friendship had known,
Parting her ways, I sought her peace alone.

Among new faces, I sought to blend,
Whispers clear, Shirin's heart won't mend.
Adapting, I found solace in change,
Moving on, in this new found range.

In the void left by Shirin, I learned to thrive,
Though tough, friends lent strength to survive.
Emotions swirled, both stormy and bright,
Through tears and laughter, I found my light.

Slowly, I embraced the change, letting go,
Bit by bit, memories softened their glow.
A new path unfolded, unfamiliar yet clear,
With each step forward, overcoming fear.

Sunshine broke through clouds of despair,
Hope blossomed anew, life beyond repair.
Adapting to absence, I grew stronger still,
In this journey onward, finding my will

Chapter – 7

I

It was not even a month without Shirin's trace,
Again she returned, messages filled with grace.
Emotions stirred as she tried to draw near,
Uncertainty lingered, hesitant to steer.

Her persistence softened my doubts strong,
Rekindling trust that had wavered long.
Slowly, I welcomed her back into my sphere,
Her presence familiar, drawing me near.

Weaving through doubts, I chose to embrace,
Forging anew, finding peace in her grace.
Together we walk, rebuilding what we knew,
With each step forward, our bond grew true

II

Afraid to risk my heart, I gave Shirin a chance,
Mature and cautious, avoiding any trance.
Careful in every step, mindful of my ways,
Liberal yet controlled, through nights and days.

Giving space, offering support, gentle and kind,
Hoping this time, true peace I would find.
Slowly, things fell into place, tentative but sure,
Apprehensions lingered, but hope endured.

Navigating uncertainties, building trust anew,
In this fragile dance, emotions grew.
A journey of healing, with each passing day,
Finding courage to trust, come what may.

III

In my darkest hour, I faltered and fell,
No longer the spark to make Shirin's heart swell.
Trying my best with remnants of old,
Yet needing her warmth in times bitter and cold.

Wishing for balance, a shared burden to bear,
But Shirin's intentions swung, she wouldn't declare.
Managing alone, nights of desperate plea,
Until frustration surged, I lost all my key.

In the moment of anguish, words spilled like rain,
For the first time, I asked her to refrain.
Out of pain or despair, it happened abrupt,
A plea from my heart, from a depth so corrupt.

IV

Alone in my darkness, grappling with pain,
Shirin, with accusations, pierced like a knife.
Accused of cheating, of contacting Navin,
I stood bewildered, wounded by strife.

For the first time, rudeness tainted my tone,
Though we ended calmly, a rift still shone.
Days of anger brewed within my chest,
Blinded by fury, I acted in unrest.

In my turmoil, emotions ran high,
I let Shirin's family breach our solitary sky.
Not a thought for right or wrong in sight,
Just rage and trauma, fuelling my fight.

But lessons learned in the harsh light of day,
Today regret echoes where anger once lay.
In loneliness' grip, clarity I find,
Seeking solace in peace of mind.

Chapter – 8

I

In the shadow of Shirin's presence, trauma grew,
Sacrifices made, paths changed, all to bid adieu.
No intention to return to what once was,
A clear line drawn, a new path chose.

Questions lingered, doubts arose,
Explanation crafted, truth in prose.
Deep was our bond, once so strong,
Now gone silent, like a forgotten song.

Struggling to appear unaffected, normalcy feigned,
Hiding turmoil, the heart's deep pain.
A new career, a fresh start in hills' embrace,
Helped heal wounds, find a peaceful space.

Now adapting to life, a new beginning found,
With courage and strength, inner peace unbound.

II

In our bubble, Shirin and I, like aliens bold,
Defied norms, in our world, our own to hold.
Untouched by reality's stormy seas,
Crafting life and emotions we please.

But when she departed, back to the norm,
I felt lost, in a world so uniform.
Struggling to adapt, feeling weak,
Daily challenges, daunting and bleak.

Life's difficulties now starkly clear,
In this world, where norms steer.
Yet I strived, though it was tough and grim,
To find my place, and peace within.

III

In the hills, I forged a new life serene,
Yet a soft corner for the old Shirin, unseen.
Memories lingered in daily life's array,
Clouds, forests, music, a nostalgic sway.

I sensed her essence in nature's embrace,
In clouds' gentle drifts, in woods' verdant grace.
In birdsong's melody, in flowers' bloom,
Kindness to all, in every small room.

Embracing nature, finding solace anew,
Becoming better, kind-hearted and true.
Her memories echoed in nights so dark,
Loneliness pierced, tears left their mark.

Yet suffocation, I learned to quell,
Shirin's story, a tale I couldn't tell.
New friends, new faces, misunderstood,
But their support, unwavering and good.

In their eyes, once more a good soul,
Hope renewed, new energy, a goal.

IV

Life was sailing smooth, adapting fine,
Then Shirin's presence, like a sign.
Her social media appearance, a bitter trace,
Leading to old frustrations, a chase.

Begged her kindly, restrict me, I pleaded,
To avoid encounters, emotions receded.
But her response, rude and so cruel,
Denial, arrogance, heart's old fuel.

Anger surged, questions arose,
For whom I've done, my efforts froze.
Out of control, no more in sway,
Lost in chaos, a different way.

V

Through my aggression intense, Siri sensed my unease,
She came to me gently, her concern on her sleeve.
"Show me your anger," she softly implored,
"Let me understand, before it spreads like a sword."

She confessed with tears, truths tangled with lies,
No soft corner remained, or so she surmised.
Yet she vowed to aid me, to mend what was torn,
To start once again, to support, from night until morn.

Emotions swelled within, I sought a peaceful end,
To reconcile our bond, and to my courage, attend.
With a heartfelt plea, I asked for her grace,
To return to us, to restore our happy place.

She accepted with a smile, a glow on her face,
Rekindling our friendship, with a new found grace.
I admitted my faults, my share in the fray,
Seeking reform, to pave a better way.

We rebuilt our rapport, with sincerity anew,
Navigating past errors, with hearts pure and true.
Respect and understanding now guided our path,
As we embraced the future, escaping the wrath
Together again, in harmony's embrace,
A testament to forgiveness, and emotion's gentle grace.

Chapter – 9

I

Once I believed in Shirin's sincere embrace,
Her support and warmth, a comforting grace.
But truth unveiled a bitter surprise,
She no longer saw me through adoring eyes.

Accepted now as flawed, not as before,
Trust and belief shattered, scattered on the floor.
Boundaries drawn, restrictions imposed,
Her old affection, now firmly closed.

The Shirin I cherished, a memory to keep,
Now distant, reserved, in boundaries deep.
Longing for the past, her warmth I miss,
But her new stance, a painful abyss.

II

Her boundaries, once tender, now thorns in my side,
More painful than her limited support, they reside.
From friend to counsellor, a shift unforeseen,
Her guidance once gentle, now feeling keen.

In the quest for closure, wounds freshly bared,
Old traumas revisited, heavy and ensnared.
Her kindness now a chain, binding my soul,
The warmth I cherished, taking its toll.

Seeking a good ending, I faced a stark truth,
Returning to hell, with memories uncouth.
Traumatized anew, I chose a path alone,
Away from her confines, forging on my own.

In solitude's embrace, I found my release,
No longer confined, finding inner peace.
Though her kindness once warmed, now stung with pain,
I'll heal from the past, and find joy again.

III

In the silence of night, secrets whisper to me,
Shirin's mysteries, locked away, yet hauntingly free.
Each memory, a thread pulling me back,
Into her world, where shadows dwell, and hearts crack.

But as time weaves its tapestry, I see,
Her indifference, her distance, no longer for me.
Why hold onto secrets that only weigh down,
When their weight is too heavy, like a silent crown?

Slowly, I unravel these tales, one by one,
Returning them to their origins, where they've begun.
For what good are memories that serve no more,
Better released, like birds to the sky, they soar.

No more suffocation, no more pain,
As I release Shirin's story, like gentle rain.
In the coming days, they'll find their place,
With those who cherish them, in time and space.

IV

In the world of words and whispered dreams,
Shirin and I found solace it seems,
Through pages turned and verses read,
Our shared emotions, unspoken, fed.

Cautious I tread, not wanting to impose,
Yet she misunderstood, I suppose,
Believed I was her beacon bright,
In her darkest hour, through her night.

Emotions ran deep, for her I cared,
No selfish reasons, just affection bared,
Confident she wouldn't depart,
Before the inevitable end, she'd stay, my heart.

Yearned for attention, to feel her near,
Significance, in her life, sincere,
A people person, surrounded wide,
Yet in her heart, a place to hide.

Amid illness and thoughts so grim,
I held her close, not to heal, but to dim,
Her burdens heavy, upon my soul,
Yet her view of me, a different role.

Mismatched emotions, tangled mess,
Planned to leave, but found no egress,
Soft corner & fate kept me anchored strong,
In her orbit, where I belong.

Partner in emotion, no reservations known,
She felt like home, where fears are sown,
Never thought her promises would break,
Only marriage, the separation we'd take.

Life's tale unfolded, unforeseen,
Complications, trauma in between,
Suffocation gripped, complexities grew,
In a whirlwind of pain, my heart she slew.

Yet through it all, lessons I find,
In the ashes of love, hopes enshrined,
For Shirin and I, our journey's crest,
A bittersweet tale, in life's tempest.

V

Tears well up as I recall,
Welcoming Shirin, standing tall,
Proud of my kindness, love I gave,
In those days, so bright and brave.

Now, tangled in misunderstanding's grasp,
Complications, trauma, an endless clasp,
Suffocation grips, emotions fray,
From beloved to the most hated today.

Her sister, most admirable, so dear,
Younger brothers, my wishes sincere,
Now they hate, despise my name,
For all of Shirin's suffering, they blame.

Alone, thoughts of past bring me pain,
Crying out loud, heart's refrain,
Their hatred, a chilling fear,
Wishing ill, their whispers sear.

Surprised at what I've become,
Strong emotions leave me numb,
Did I deserve such disdain?
Or forgiveness, a chance to regain?

Questioning the Almighty's plan,
Was I truly so flawed, a broken man?
Shirin knew my faults, yet she came,
Promised solace, yet now blames.

In being cast as the villain's role,
I find solace, peace for my soul,
No longer suffocating, no loss of pride,
I'm free to choose, to decide

After trauma's trials, I stand tall,
No obligation to kindness, after all,
Gave my best, tried with might,
Now free to do what feels right.

VI

In the quiet moments of my days, I see,
The pain I felt, a lesson meant for me.
Shirin's shadow brought a heavy storm,
A punishment I couldn't then transform.

I never grasped the warmth of being close,
Or how to stand beside, a friend engrossed.
Ignoring love that tried to find my heart,
I laughed at feelings that set souls apart.

Yet now I see the truth in all the strife,
A mirror showing the regrets of life.

VII

In dreams, Shirin's smile from clouds above,
Guides me gently with her lasting love.
She was a soul in human guise, now set free,
Merged with nature, in eternal harmony.

I sense her presence in the whispering breeze,
Guiding me through life's complexities.
Her essence brings luck, in tough times she's near,
A phase of love and soul, forever dear.

No one can steal these memories we share,
For love tanscends, beyond earthly fare.

An Ode To Kotdwar

In Kotdwar's embrace, my heart finds peace,
Where the railway station's echoes release.
Through joys and pains, it stands witness true,
To every emotion I've journeyed through.

From happiness bright to excitement's glow,
Smiles and thrills and nerves that flow.
Heartbreak's ache and the sting of tears,
Feelings ignored, and desperate fears.

Yet amidst it all, this place has known,
The real me, emotions freely shown.-
From meeting love in an adorable glance,
To the sorrow of waiting, left by chance.

This station, once broken, now renewed,
With modern grace and hope pursued.
But oh, those old walls, dear and true,
Where memories of us still imbue.

In Kotdwar's railway station, forever remains,
The beauty of moments, joy and pains.
A sanctuary where my story's told,
In the echoes of love, and memories old.

About the Author

Arnav Vibhuti

Arnav Vibhuti was born in Darbhanga, Bihar, and works as a government servant. He holds a Master's degree in Sociology and is an active member of Navodaya Mission, an NGO dedicated to uplifting tribal children. Arnav's writing career began with diary entries during his school days, which blossomed into a passion for blogging. With a deep love for storytelling and expressing emotions through words, he uses his literary skills to convey powerful narratives and emotional journeys.

www.ingramcontent.com/pod-product-compliance
Lightning Source LLC
LaVergne TN
LVHW041553070526
838199LV00046B/1950